Team Spirit

THE MIAMI DOLPHINS

BY

MARK STEWART

Content Consultant
Jason Aikens
Collections Curator
The Professional Football Hall of Fame

NORWOOD HOUSE PRESS

CHICAGO, ILLINOIS

Norwood House Press
P.O. Box 316598
Chicago, Illinois 60631

For information regarding Norwood House Press, please visit our website at:
www.norwoodhousepress.com or call 866-565-2900.

PHOTO CREDITS:
All photos courtesy of AP Images—AP/Wide World Photos, Inc. except the following:
Topps, Inc. (7, 14, 17 bottom, 18, 20, 21, 22 both,
34 both, 39, 40 both & 43); John Klein (23 top, 35 right & 41 left);
PhotoFest (28 & 37); Author's collection (41 top and bottom).
Special thanks to Topps, Inc.

Editor: Mike Kennedy
Designer: Ron Jaffe
Project Management: Black Book Partners, LLC.
Special thanks to Laura Peabody and Liz Pearson.

LIBRARY OF CONGRESS CATALOGING-IN-PUBLICATION DATA

Stewart, Mark, 1960-
   The Miami Dolphins / by Mark Stewart ; with content consultant Jason
Aikens.
      p. cm. -- (Team spirit)
   Summary: "Presents the history, accomplishments and key personalities of
the Miami Dolphins football team. Includes timelines, quotes, maps, glos-
sary and websites"--Provided by publisher.
   Includes bibliographical references and index.
   ISBN-13: 978-1-59953-065-9 (library edition : alk. paper)
   ISBN-10: 1-59953-065-1 (library edition : alk. paper)
   1. Miami Dolphins (Football team)--History--Juvenile literature. I.
Aikens, Jason. II. Title. III. Series: Stewart, Mark, 1960- Team spirit.
   GV956.M47S74 2007
   796.332'6409759381--dc22
                                                    2006015337

COVER PHOTO: The Dolphins celebrate a fumble recovery
and touchdown in a 2005 victory over the Buffalo Bills.

Table of Contents

SPORTS WORDS & VOCABULARY WORDS: In this book, you will find many words that are new to you. You may also see familiar words used in new ways. The glossary on page 46 gives the meanings of football words, as well as "everyday" words that have special football meanings. These words appear in **bold type** throughout the book. The glossary on page 47 gives the meanings of vocabulary words that are not related to football. They appear in ***bold italic type*** throughout the book.

Meet the Dolphins

The Miami area is home to millionaires, movie stars, and music legends. There are young people who love the warm weather and long, sandy beaches. Many older people move to this part of Florida when they retire. And, of course, there are thousands of people who work hard at different jobs and like to spend time with their friends and family. All of these people have one thing in common—each year, when football season comes, they root for the Miami Dolphins.

The Dolphins were the first **professional** team to find success in Miami. The city's fans love them for this, and support them whether they win or lose. The players return this love by giving everything they have whenever they take the field.

This book tells the story of the Dolphins. The fans may treat them like *celebrities* when they see them on the streets of Miami, but on Sundays they are the hardest-working guys in town.

Marty Booker and Chris Chambers celebrate
a touchdown during the 2005 season.

Way Back When

Professional football was not always the popular sport it is today. During the 1950s, however, this began to change. A new league called the **American Football League (AFL)** began in 1960. The AFL had eight teams, with most located in cities that did not have teams in the older **National Football League (NFL)**. Soon, fans all over the United States wanted their own team.

Joe Foss, the ***commissioner*** of the AFL, thought Miami would make a fine place for a new team. He knew that Joe Robbie, a

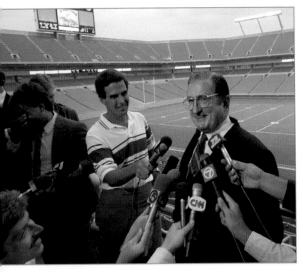

powerful ***lawyer***, wanted to own one. Foss suggested to Robbie that he find some partners to ***invest*** in an AFL team that would play in the fast-growing Florida city. Robbie and a group that included a television star named Danny Thomas became the owners of the Miami Dolphins. They played their first game in 1966.

The Dolphins built their team by selecting extra players from other AFL clubs. They also **drafted** college players. The Dolphins

ABOVE: Team owner Joe Robbie gives an interview.
RIGHT: Larry Csonka

won only three games their first year, and had very bad luck with their quarterbacks. So many were injured that the coach, George Wilson, ended up using his son at quarterback!

Over the next few years, the Dolphins drafted a group of good young players that included Bob Griese, Larry Csonka, Howard Twilley, Dick Anderson, Jim Kiick, and Mercury Morris. Miami also traded for older stars Nick Buonionti, Paul Warfield, and Bob Matheson. In 1970, the team hired Don Shula, one of the best coaches in football. In only his second season, the Dolphins made it all the way to the **Super Bowl**.

The Dolphins became one of the best teams in history. They returned to the Super Bowl twice during the 1970s and won both times. In 1972, the Dolphins won all 14 games during the regular season, and then three more postseason games—including Super Bowl VII—to become the first team to finish with a perfect 17–0 record.

The team succeeded because each player worked hard and did his job well. Most football fans in the 1970s did not know much about people like Jim Langer, Larry Little, Bob Kuechenberg, Manny Fernandez, Bill Stanfill, and Vern Den Herder, but Miami's

opponents sure knew who they were. The same was true years later, when the Dolphins were led by A.J. Duhe, Bob Baumhower, Dwight Stephenson, Ed Newman, Duriel Harris, Andra Franklin, and David Woodley. They were champions of the **American Football Conference (AFC)** in 1982, but lost to the Washington Redskins in Super Bowl XVII.

The Dolphins hoped that a new quarterback would change their luck. They drafted strong-armed Dan Marino, who led them back to the Super Bowl two years later. During a long and brilliant career, Marino smashed almost every passing record.

However, he never led the Dolphins to another Super Bowl.

Coach Shula retired in 1996, and Marino left football four seasons later. The Dolphins looked for new leaders, and found them in a pair of hard-hitting tacklers named Zach Thomas and Jason Taylor. Like the stars who wore the Miami uniform before them, they got the job done without being flashy, and *inspired* their teammates to give everything they had on every play.

LEFT: Dan Marino scans the field for an open receiver.
RIGHT: Don Shula talks things over with Dan Marino.

The Team Today

The Dolphins win games the old-fashioned way. They mix smart, experienced players with young, exciting ones. They try to find quality people to play each position, and work as a team to beat their opponents. Although the Dolphins have had many great stars over the years, they understand that a winning play is often made by a **substitute** or **specials-teams player**.

The goal for the Dolphins is to build a balanced team. They look for quarterbacks that can make short passes or throw long bombs. They have a mix of **receivers**—some can get open with their speed alone, while others catch passes with sharp cuts and sure hands. Miami's running attack depends on good **blocking** and *precise* timing.

The Miami defense also looks for balance. The Dolphins teach their tacklers to recognize what an opponent is trying to do, and then how to react quickly.

The Dolphins are not expected to have a perfect season, as the 1972 team did. However, each player knows that he must honor the Dolphins of the past by working hard and giving his best effort.

Randy McMichael gives Chris Chambers a hug.
The Dolphins have great team pride and spirit.

Home Turf

The Dolphins play their home games in Dolphins Stadium, which is located about 30 minutes northwest of downtown Miami. It is one of the most *luxurious* sports arenas in the United States.

Dolphins Stadium opened in 1987. For a while, it was named Joe Robbie Stadium, after the team's first owner. Besides being the team's home, the stadium is often used by the NFL for the Super Bowl.

Every seat in Dolphins Stadium has a great view of the field. If fans happen to miss a play, they can always watch an instant replay on the large television screens located at each end of the field.

DOLPHINS STADIUM BY THE NUMBERS

- *Dolphins Stadium has 75,000 seats.*
- *Dolphins Stadium cost $115 million to build in 1987.*
- *The Dolphins opened the stadium with a preseason game against the Chicago Bears on August 16, 1987. Miami lost 10–3.*

The Dolphins' home stadium is pictured prior to Super Bowl XXIX in 1995. The San Francisco 49ers and San Diego Chargers played in this game.

Dressed for Success

The Dolphins' team colors are aqua green, coral orange, blue, and white. Their *logo* is a dolphin in front of an orange sunburst. The Miami helmet is white, with green and orange stripes running down the middle, and the dolphin logo on each side. There have been a few small changes over the years, but the basic uniform looks very much the same as it did in 1966.

FRANK EMANUEL
MIAMI DOLPHINS
LINEBACKER

The Dolphins usually wear one of two color combinations. At home, the team prefers aqua green jerseys and white pants, with coral orange trim. When the Dolphins play on the road, they normally flip-flop their colors, with white jerseys and aqua green pants.

This 1968 trading card of Frank Emanuel shows the Dolphins' early uniform and the team logo.

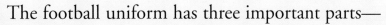

The football uniform has three important parts—

- Helmet
- Jersey
- Pants

Helmets used to be made out of leather, and they did not have facemasks—ouch! Today, helmets are made of super-strong plastic. The uniform top, or jersey, is made of thick fabric. It fits snugly around a player so that tacklers cannot grab it and pull him down. The pants come down just over the knees.

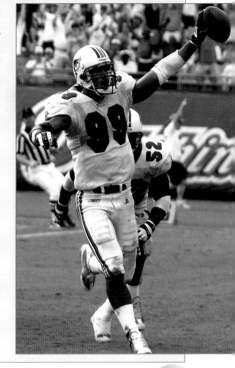

There is a lot more to a football uniform than what you see on the outside. Air can be pumped inside the helmet to give it a snug, padded fit. The jersey covers shoulder pads, and sometimes a rib-protector called a "flak jacket." The pants include pads that protect the hips, thighs, *tailbone*, and knees.

Football teams have two sets of uniforms—one dark and one light. This makes it easier to tell two teams apart on the field. Almost all teams wear their dark uniforms at home, and their light ones on the road.

Jason Taylor scores a touchdown for the defense. His shoulder and thigh pads can be seen in this photo.

We Won!

The Dolphins played their first season in 1966, and finished in last place. Five seasons later, they found themselves in the **AFC Championship** against the Baltimore Colts. The Dolphins won 21–0 to earn a spot in Super Bowl VI, but their amazing run ended when they lost to the Cowboys 24–3.

One season later, in 1972, the Dolphins did something truly extraordinary. They went through the entire regular season without losing a single game. It was a true team effort. Bob Griese, the

team's star quarterback, broke his leg early in the season. Coach Don Shula convinced his players that they could win without Griese. He made 38-year-old Earl Morrall his quarterback, and the Dolphins continued to win game after game.

After finishing the year 14–0, the Dolphins defeated the Cleveland Browns and Pittsburgh Steelers in exciting **playoff games**. Griese returned from his injury in time to lead the Dolphins in Super VII against the Washington Redskins.

The young Dolphins had three excellent runners in Larry Csonka, Jim Kiick, and Mercury Morris. What made the team great, however, was the defense. It was led by Manny Fernandez, Nick Buoniconti, and Jake Scott. They were called the "No-Name" defense because few fans outside of Florida were familiar with the Miami players.

In the Super Bowl, the Washington offense struggled to make first downs, and went the entire game without scoring a field goal or touchdown. The only points Washington made came on a defensive play late in the game. The Dolphins scored touchdowns on a pass from Griese to Howard Twilley, and a short run by Kiick. The final score was 14–7. The star of the game was Scott, who **intercepted** two passes.

LEFT: Larry Csonka and Jim Kiick
TOP RIGHT: Manny Fernandez   **BOTTOM RIGHT**: Bob Griese

The Dolphins returned to the Super Bowl a year later. They finished the 1973 season 12–2, and then beat the Cincinnati Bengals and Oakland Raiders in the playoffs. Just as they had the year before, the Dolphins used their running backs to wear down their opponents, and relied on their defense to keep other teams from scoring.

DOLPHINS 24 VIKINGS 7

★ SUPERBOWL VIII ★

In Super Bowl VIII, Miami played a very similar team, the Minnesota Vikings. In this battle of defenses, the winner was Csonka, who put his head down and plowed his way to 145 yards and two touchdowns. Minnesota's star running back, Chuck Foreman, gained only 18 yards against the "No-Names."

Miami fans believed their team would win many more Super Bowls. Although the Dolphins returned to the big game twice more, they did not find the championship magic again. In Super Bowl XVII—a rematch with the Redskins—the Dolphins were ahead 13–10 in the fourth quarter, but could not hold the lead. In Super Bowl XIX, Miami's Dan Marino and Joe Montana of the San Francisco 49ers each passed for more than 300 yards, but the 49ers *triumphed* 38–16.

Were the Miami Dolphins of the early 1970s the greatest team ever? Many football experts believe that they were. The team won 32 times during the 1972 and 1973 seasons, and only lost twice. They not only beat good teams in back-to-back Super Bowls, they *dominated* those teams.

LEFT: This trading card shows Larry Csonka running against the Vikings in Super Bowl VIII.   **RIGHT**: Minnesota quarterback Fran Tarkenton is sandwiched by the "No-Name" defense.

Go-To Guys

To be a true star in the NFL, you need more than fast feet and a big body. You have to be a "go-to guy"—someone the coach wants on the field at the end of a big game. Dolphins fans have had a lot to cheer about over the years, including these great stars…

THE PIONEERS

Bob Griese

BOB GRIESE — Quarterback

• BORN: 2/3/1945 • PLAYED FOR TEAM: 1967 TO 1980

Bob Griese was the team's first true star. He was a smart leader and an **accurate** passer who understood how to use all of Miami's weapons.

LARRY CSONKA — Running Back

• BORN: 12/25/1946 • PLAYED FOR TEAM: 1968 TO 1974 AND 1979

Larry Csonka could run around tacklers, and he could run *over* them. The defensive players of the 1970s say that no one was harder to bring down.

NICK BUONICONTI — Linebacker

• BORN: 12/15/1940 • PLAYED FOR TEAM: 1969 TO 1974 AND 1976

Nick Buoniconti was the heart of the "No-Name" defense. He was a hard tackler who played like every down was his last.

PAUL WARFIELD   Receiver

- Born: 11/28/1942   • Played for Team: 1970 to 1974

Paul Warfield was Miami's most dangerous weapon. When opponents tried to crowd their defense around the Dolphins' runners, Warfield would catch long passes to break open close games. He averaged more than 20 yards per catch for the team.

JAKE SCOTT   Safety

- Born: 7/20/1945   • Played for Team: 1970 to 1975

Jake Scott drove Miami's opponents crazy. He always seemed to be in the right place at the right time—for a bone-crunching tackle or a *spectacular* interception.

LARRY LITTLE   Guard

- Born: 11/2/1945
- Played for Team: 1969 to 1980

Larry Little was the key blocker on many of the Dolphins' running plays. He was strong enough to push his man straight off the **line of scrimmage** on inside runs, and quick enough to pull away from his guard position and lead the blocking on outside runs.

LEFT: Bob Griese   **ABOVE**: Larry Little

DWIGHT STEPHENSON   Center

• BORN: 11/20/1957 • PLAYED FOR TEAM: 1980 TO 1987

It took a season for Dwight Stephenson to win a starting job with the Dolphins, but once he was given a chance he proved to be one of the best centers in history. He was voted **All-Pro** five years in a row.

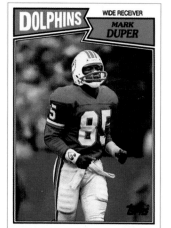

MARK DUPER   Receiver

• BORN: 1/25/1959

• PLAYED FOR TEAM: 1982 TO 1992

Mark Duper had incredible speed, and often zoomed right past **defensive backs** on **fly patterns**. He and Mark Clayton were nicknamed the "Marks Brothers."

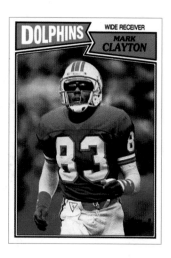

MARK CLAYTON   Receiver

• BORN: 4/8/1961

• PLAYED FOR TEAM: 1983 TO 1992

Mark Clayton was quick and *crafty*. He was an expert at getting open, and was extremely hard to tackle once he caught the ball. In 1984, Clayton caught 18 touchdown passes.

TOP: Mark Duper
BOTTOM: Mark Clayton

DAN MARINO   Quarterback

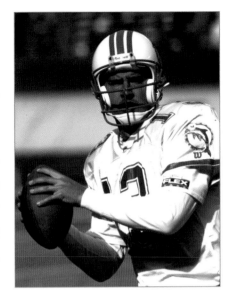

- BORN: 9/15/1961
- PLAYED FOR TEAM: 1983 TO 1999

Many football experts consider Dan Marino to be the best quarterback ever. He released the ball so quickly and threw with such accuracy that he changed the way NFL defenses were designed. In 1984, Marino threw for 48 touchdowns and over 5,000 yards.

ZACH THOMAS   Linebacker

- BORN: 9/1/1973   • FIRST SEASON WITH TEAM: 1996

No one predicted that Zach Thomas would become a star when the Dolphins drafted him. He was smaller and slower than other middle linebackers, but he worked twice as hard to become one of the best in the NFL.

JASON TAYLOR   Defensive End

- BORN: 9/1/1974
- FIRST SEASON WITH TEAM: 1997

Miami fans have compared speedy Jason Taylor to a guided missile. Once he gets a running back or quarterback in his sights, chances are good that he will score a direct hit. In 2002, Taylor set a team record with 18.5 **sacks**.

TOP: Dan Marino
BOTTOM: Jason Taylor

On the Sidelines

For 26 years, the man roaming the sidelines for the Miami Dolphins was Don Shula. He won 347 games, more than any coach in history. Shula came to the Dolphins after winning a championship with the Colts. As the leader of the Dolphins, he won 266 games. He led the team to the Super Bowl in each of his first three seasons, and five times in all.

Shula set the *standard* for all of the Miami coaches that followed him. He paid close attention to detail, and was an expert at *motivating* every player on the team—from his stars to his substitutes. Shula demanded that his players work hard in practice and that they stay focused on their duties during games.

In 2005, Miami hired Nick Saban to coach the Dolphins. Like Shula, Saban came to the team with a great winning record. As a college coach, he led Louisiana State University to the **National Championship**. The Dolphins still dedicate themselves to Shula's *tradition* of excellence.

Don Shula is all smiles during a 25th anniversary celebration for the 1972 Dolphins.

One Great Day

When Miami Dolphins fans settled in front of their televisions on Christmas Day in 1971, they were all wishing for the same gift: The team's first-ever playoff victory. It would not be easy. They were playing the Kansas City Chiefs—the Super Bowl champions two years earlier—at Arrowhead Stadium in Kansas City.

Both teams had star-studded lineups. Naturally everyone believed that the game would come down to a great play by Miami's Bob Griese or Larry Csonka, or Kansas City's Len Dawson or Otis Taylor. Little did anyone think that the game would come down to a duel of kickers!

Jan Stenerud of the Chiefs (from Norway) and Miami's Garo Yepremian (from Cyprus) were former soccer players making a living booting balls in the NFL. In this game they were called upon time and again to provide their team with *crucial* points.

The Chiefs led 10–0 in the first quarter, but the Dolphins fought back to tie the score at halftime. Kansas City scored touchdowns in the third and fourth quarters. Each time, Miami scored to tie

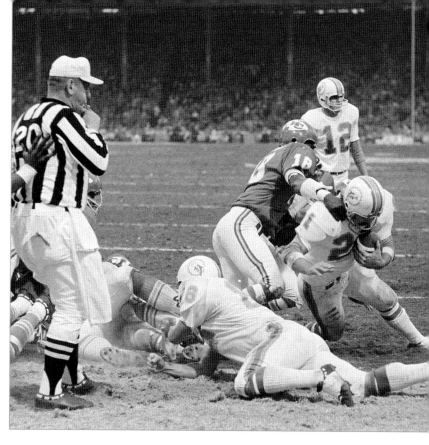

Jim Kiick scores a touchdown for the Dolphins against the Chiefs during their 1971 playoff game.

the game again. The Chiefs had a chance to win as time ran out, but Stenerud's kick sailed wide of the goal posts and the game went into **overtime** knotted 24–24.

The Chiefs moved quickly to end the game, **driving** deep into Miami territory. Stenerud tried another field goal, but Nick Buoniconti saved the day for the Dolphins by blocking the kick. Neither team scored during the 15-minute extra period, so for the first time in history an NFL game went into double-overtime.

Finally, halfway through the second extra period, Miami drove to Kansas City's 30 yard line. Yepremian, the smallest player on the field, made the biggest kick of his life. His **field goal** from the 37 yard line tumbled over the crossbar to give the Dolphins a 27–24 victory in the longest game ever played.

Legend Has It

Who was the best actor in Dolphins history?

LEGEND HAS IT that it was Dan Marino. In 1994, he played himself in *Ace Ventura: Pet Detective*, which starred Jim Carrey. He also appeared in *Holy Man* with Eddie Murphy, and the music video "Only Wanna Be With You" by Hootie and the Blowfish.

Were the Dolphins almost named the Sharks?

LEGEND HAS IT that they were. In 1965, Miami's owners held a contest to name the team. Nearly 20,000 entries were received. Among the names suggested were the Mariners, Marauders, Mustangs, Missiles, and Moons. With 622 votes, the Dolphins just beat the Sharks. Mrs. Robert Swanson of West Miami won the contest, and earned two lifetime passes to the team's games.

Who was the worst passer in Dolphins history?

LEGEND HAS IT that it was Garo Yepremian—a place kicker! Toward the end of Super Bowl VII, the tiny Yepremian was ready to try a field goal against the Washington Redskins. The ball squirted loose from the **holder's** grasp, however, and Yepremian picked it up only to realize that the entire Washington defense was charging at him. He had never actually thrown a pass in his life, but this seemed like a good time for his first one. Yepremian's arm went forward, but unfortunately the ball just popped straight in the air. Mike Bass of the Redskins caught it and ran 49 yards for a touchdown.

LEFT: Dan Marino is all tied up in this scene with Jim Carrey.
ABOVE: Karl Noonan holds the ball for Garo Yepremian. Yepremian should have been practicing his passes!

It Really Happened

Have you ever heard the saying "nobody's perfect?" Well, don't tell the 1972 Dolphins that. The team won every game it played that season, including two playoff wins and a victory in Super Bowl VII.

The key to this amazing record may have been a move the team made many months before the season started. Coach Don Shula wanted an experienced back-up for his star quarterback, Bob Griese, so he signed 38-year-old Earl Morrall. Years earlier, when Shula coached the Baltimore Colts, Morrall had filled in after Johnny Unitas was injured, and the team made it to the Super Bowl. If anything happened to Griese, Shula wanted Morrall on his side.

As luck would have it, Griese *was* injured. After leading the Dolphins to four victories, he broke his leg against the San Diego Chargers. Shula made Morrall the starter, and he led the Dolphins to a 24–23 win the following Sunday. The week after that, the Dolphins shutout the Colts 23–0.

Everyone tried extra-hard knowing that they had an "old man" at quarterback. The Miami defense played brilliantly all year, and the Dolphins' runners had one great game after another. Meanwhile, Morrall surprised everyone by becoming the AFC's top-rated passer!

The Dolphins could do no wrong. They finished the season with a second **shutout** of the Colts to end up 14–0. In the first round of the playoffs, the Miami defense intercepted five passes against the Cleveland Browns to win 20–14. In the AFC Championship against the Pittsburgh Steelers, Griese replaced Morrall with the score tied 7–7 and won the game 21–17.

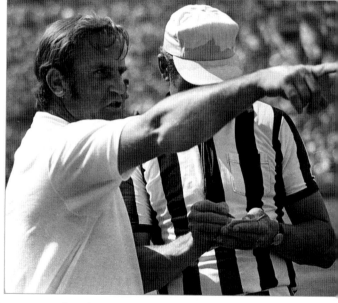

With just the Super Bowl standing between them and the NFL's first perfect record, the Dolphins beat the Washington Redskins in the big game 14–7. After the season, Shula admitted he was nervous before the Super Bowl. If the Dolphins had lost and finished 16–1 instead of 17–0, he knew that their great season would soon be forgotten.

LEFT: Earl Morrall, the hero of Miami's undefeated season.
ABOVE: Don Shula makes his point with a referee.

Team Spirit

The weather in Miami can be beautiful when autumn comes each year. On the weekends, people love to go outside and enjoy the sunshine. For 75,000 Miami football fans, there is no better place to see the "fall colors" than at Dolphins Stadium, where aqua green and coral orange hats, jerseys, and pennants fill the stands.

When the Dolphins are scoring points and making tackles, the stadium comes alive with energy and excitement. If you listen closely, you may also hear some noise when the visiting team is doing well. Miami is home to people from all over the country, and many come to Dolphins games to root for their old hometown teams—just not too loudly!

Win or lose, going to a Dolphins game is always entertaining. The team has one of the best cheerleading squads in the NFL, and T.D. the Miami mascot always keeps fans smiling as he roams the sidelines.

LEFT: Donald Lee "high-fives" the fans at Dolphins Stadium.
ABOVE: Jay Fiedler lets the fans know he hears their cheers.

Timeline

In this timeline, each Super Bowl is listed under the year it was played. Remember that the Super Bowl is held early in the year, and is actually part of the previous season. For example, Super Bowl XL was played on February 4 of 2006, but it was the championship of the 2005 NFL season.

1966
The Dolphins play their first season.

1974
The Dolphins defeat the Minnesota Vikings in Super Bowl VIII.

1967
Rookie Jack Clancy finishes second in the AFL with 67 catches.

1970
The Dolphins sign coach Don Shula.

1973
The Dolphins defeat the Washington Redskins in Super Bowl VII.

Jack Clancy

Jake Scott, MVP of Super Bowl VII.

Dan
Marino

Don
Shula

1984
Dan Marino throws 48
touchdown passes.

1996
Don Shula retires with a
record 347 career victories.

1983
The Dolphins
play in Super
Bowl XVII but
lose to the
Redskins.

1989
The Dolphins move from
the Orange Bowl to their
current home.

2004
Zach Thomas
plays in his fourth
Pro Bowl.

David Woodley,
the quarterback who led
Miami to Super Bowl XVII.

Fun Facts

NICE START

In 1966, Joe Auer returned the opening kickoff of the Dolphins' first game for a 95-yard touchdown against the Oakland Raiders.

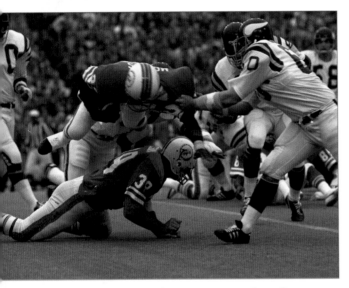

DOUBLE TROUBLE

In 1972, Larry Csonka and Mercury Morris became the first teammates to rush for 1,000 yards each in the same season.

ALL OR NOTHING

Linebacker Larry Ball is the only player in history to play for an undefeated team and a winless team. He was on the 17–0 Dolphins in 1972, and then joined Tampa Bay in 1976. The Buccaneers went 0–14 that season.

BE NICE TO MY SISTER

Jason Taylor's wife, Katrina, is the sister of teammate Zach Thomas.

FAST FREDDIE

In a 1976 game, Freddie Solomon scored three touchdowns for the Dolphins—one on a 79-yard punt return, another on a 53-yard pass play, and another on a 59-yard run.

TV STARS

After leading Miami to victory in Super Bowl VII, Jim Kiick and Larry Csonka were invited to appear on *The Tonight Show.*

WORLD STAGE

The Dolphins are extremely popular with sports fans outside the United States. They have often been invited to play in the American Bowl, an NFL exhibition game held each year in different countries around the world.

STORMY WEATHER

The Dolphins have had two games cancelled because of hurricanes—Hurricane Andrew in 1992 and Hurricane Ivan in 2004.

LEFT: Mercury Morris dives over his teammate, Larry Csonka.
ABOVE: Larry Conka and Jim Kiick talk to Johnny Carson on *The Tonight Show.*

Talking Football

"Success is not forever and failure isn't fatal."
—*Don Shula, on dealing with winning and losing in football*

"There is no defense against a perfect pass. I can throw the perfect pass."
—*Dan Marino, on what made him a great quarterback*

"There might be one or two catches where I'm like, 'Man—I can't believe I caught that!' But I've kind of gotten used to it."
—*Chris Chambers, on his amazing diving catches*

"When I was playing and practicing in that heat in July and August in Miami with shoulder pads on, I would just **vaporize**."

—*Larry Csonka, on surviving training camp with the Dolphins*

"I guess I'm a **relic** from the past. But I still believe football is a team sport. I still believe you have to respect your teammates."

—*Paul Warfield, on the true essence of football*

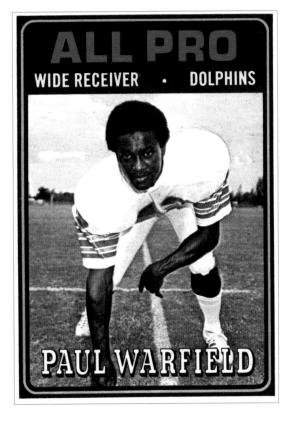

ALL PRO

WIDE RECEIVER • DOLPHINS

PAUL WARFIELD

"There was something very special about the '72 and '73 Dolphins…How many teams can claim a record of 32–2? In the entire history of the game, that team was unique."

—*Bob Griese, on Miami's Super Bowl champions*

"It's great playing with family…being together so long, as two leaders of the team, that's pretty uncommon."

—*Zach Thomas, on playing beside his brother-in-law, Jason Taylor, for so many seasons*

LEFT: Dan Marino   **ABOVE**: Paul Warfield

For the Record

The great Dolphins teams and players have left their marks on the record books. These are the "best of the best"…

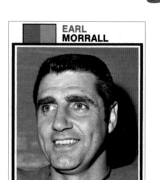

Earl Morrall

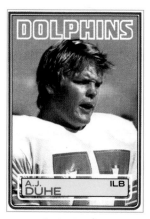

A.J. Duhe

DOLPHINS AWARD WINNERS

WINNER	AWARD	YEAR
Don Shula	AFC Coach of the Year	1970
Don Shula	AFC Coach of the Year	1971
Don Shula	NFL Coach of the Year	1972
Earl Morrall	Comeback Player of the Year	1972
Jake Scott	Super Bowl VII MVP	1973
Garo Yepremian	Pro Bowl Most Valuable Player	1973
Dick Anderson	NFL Defensive Player of the Year	1973
Larry Csonka	Super Bowl VIII MVP	1974
A.J. Duhe	NFL Defensive Rookie of the Year	1977
Larry Csonka	Comeback Player of the Year	1979
Doug Betters	NFL Defensive Player of the Year	1983
Dan Marino	AFC Offensive Player of the Year	1984
Dan Marino	NFL Most Valuable Player	1984
Troy Stradford	NFL Offensive Rookie of the Year	1987
Richmond Webb	AFC Rookie of the Year	1990
Tim Bowens	NFL Defensive Rookie of the Year	1994
Dan Marino	Comeback Player of the Year	1994
Ricky Williams	Pro Bowl Most Valuable Player	2003

DOLPHINS ACHIEVEMENTS

ACHIEVEMENT	YEAR
AFC Champions	1971
AFC Champions	1972
Super Bowl VII Champions	1972*
AFC Champions	1973
Super Bowl VIII Champions	1973*
AFC East Champions	1974
AFC East Champions	1979
AFC East Champions	1981
AFC Champions	1982
AFC East Champions	1983
AFC Champions	1984
AFC East Champions	1985
AFC East Champions	1992
AFC East Champions	1994
AFC East Champions	2000

Super Bowls are played early the following year, but the game is counted as the championship of this season.

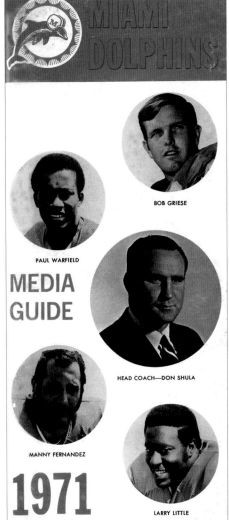

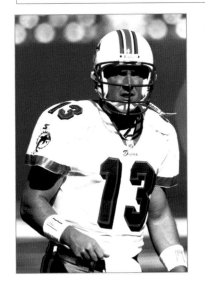

TOP RIGHT: Don Shula and four Miami stars were featured on the cover of the team's 1971 guide book. **ABOVE**: A pennant celebrating Miami's trip to Super Bowl XVII. **LEFT**: Dan Marino, the NFL's MVP in 1984.

Pinpoints

T he history of a football team is made up of many smaller stories. These stories take place all over the map—not just in the city a team calls "home." Match the push-pins on these maps to the Team Facts and you will begin to see the story of the Dolphins unfold!

TEAM FACTS

1 Miami, Florida—*The Dolphins play their home games here.*

2 Springfield, Massachusetts—*Nick Buoniconti was born here.*

3 Grand River, Ohio—*Don Shula was born here.*

4 Pittsburgh, Pennsylvania—*Dan Marino was born here.*

5 Evansville, Indiana—*Bob Griese was born here.*

6 New Orleans, Louisiana—*A.J. Duhe was born here.*

7 Pampa, Texas—*Zach Thomas was born here.*

8 Los Angeles, California—*The Dolphins won Super Bowl VII here.*

9 London, England—*The Dolphins played their first American Bowl here.*

10 Tokyo, Japan—*The Dolphins played their second American Bowl here.*

11 Berlin, Germany—*The Dolphins played their third American Bowl here.*

12 Larnaca, Cyprus—*Garo Yepremian was born here*

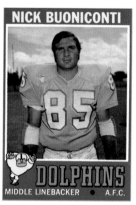

Nick Buoniconti

43

Play Ball

Football is a sport played by two teams on a field that is 100 yards long. The game is divided into four 15-minute quarters. Each team must have 11 players on the field at all times. The group that has the ball is called the offense. The group trying to keep the offense from moving the ball forward is called the defense.

A football game is made up of a series of "plays." Each play starts and ends with a referee's signal. A play begins when the center snaps the ball between his legs to the quarterback. The quarterback then gives the ball to a teammate, throws (or "passes") the ball to a teammate, or runs with the ball himself. The job of the defense is to tackle the player with the ball or stop the quarterback's pass. A play ends when the ball (or player holding the ball) is "down." The offense must move the ball forward at least 10 yards every four downs. If it fails to do so, the other team is given the ball. If the offense has not made 10 yards after three downs—and does not want to risk losing the ball—it can kick (or "punt") the ball to make the other team start from its own end of the field.

At each end of a football field is a goal line, which divides the field from the end zone. A team must run or pass the ball over the goal line to score a touchdown, which counts for six points. After scoring a touchdown, a team can try a short kick for one "extra point," or try again to run or pass across the goal line for two points. Teams can score three points from anywhere on the field by kicking the ball between the goal posts. This is called a field goal.

The defense can score two points if it tackles a player while he is in his own end zone. This is called a safety. The defense can also score points by taking the ball away from the offense and crossing the opposite goal line for a touchdown. The team with the most points after 60 minutes is the winner.

Football may seem like a very hard game to understand, but the more you play and watch football, the more "little things" you are likely to notice. The next time you are at a game, look for these plays:

PLAY LIST

BLITZ—A play where the defense sends extra tacklers after the quarterback. If the quarterback sees a blitz coming, he passes the ball quickly. If he does not, he can end up on the bottom of a very big pile!

DRAW—A play where the offense pretends it will pass the ball, and then gives it to a running back. If the offense can "draw" the defense to the quarterback and his receivers, the running back should have lots of room to run.

FLY PATTERN—A play where a team's fastest receiver is told to "fly" past the defensive backs for a long pass. Many long touchdowns are scored on this play.

SQUIB KICK—A play where the ball is kicked a short distance on purpose. A squib kick is used when the team kicking off does not want the other team's fastest player to catch the ball and run with it.

SWEEP—A play where the ball-carrier follows a group of teammates moving sideways to "sweep" the defense out of the way. A good sweep gives the runner a chance to gain a lot of yards before he is tackled or forced out of bounds.

Glossary

FOOTBALL WORDS TO KNOW

AFC CHAMPIONSHIP—The game played to decide which American Football Conference team will go to the Super Bowl.

ALL-PRO—An honor given to the best players at their position at the end of each season. A "first-team" All-Pro is someone who is voted the best of the best.

AMERICAN FOOTBALL CONFERENCE (AFC)—One of two groups of teams that make up the National Football League (NFL). The winner of the AFC plays the winner of the National Football Conference (NFC) in the Super Bowl.

AMERICAN FOOTBALL LEAGUE (AFL)—The football league that began play in 1960, and later merged with the National Football League (NFL).

BLOCKING—Using the body to protect a teammate who has the ball.

DEFENSIVE BACKS—Players who play "back" on defense, such as cornerbacks and safeties.

DRAFTED—Selected from a group of the best college players.

DRIVING—Pushing the defense back toward its own goal.

FIELD GOAL—A goal from the field, kicked over the crossbar and between the goal posts. A field goal is worth three points.

FLY PATTERNS—Pass plays that call for a receiver to "fly" down the field, past the defense.

HOLDER—The player whose job is to hold the ball in place for the kicker.

INTERCEPTED—Caught by a defensive player.

LINE OF SCRIMMAGE—The imaginary line where each play starts.

NATIONAL CHAMPIONSHIP—The honor given to the best team in college football at the end of each season.

NATIONAL FOOTBALL LEAGUE (NFL)—The league that started in 1920 and still operates today.

OVERTIME—The period played to decide the winner of a game that is tied after 60 minutes. This period is sometimes called "sudden death" because the game ends as soon as one team scores.

PLAYOFF GAMES—The games played after the season that determine which teams meet in the Super Bowl.

PROFESSIONAL—A person or team that plays a sport for money. College players are not paid, so they are considered "amateurs."

RECEIVERS—Players who catch a quarterback's passes.

ROOKIE—A player in his first season.

SACKS—A statistic that measures how many times the quarterback is tackled for a loss.

SHUTOUT—A game in which a team does not allow its opponent to score.

SPECIAL-TEAMS PLAYER—A player who takes the field for special plays, including kickoffs, punts, and field goals.

SUBSTITUTE—Someone who fills in for another player.

SUPER BOWL—The championship game of football, played between the winner of the American Football Conference (AFC) and the National Football Conference (NFC).

OTHER WORDS TO KNOW

ACCURATE—Free of mistakes and errors.

CELEBRITIES—People who are very famous.

COMMISSIONER—The head of a group.

CRAFTY—Sly or cunning.

CRUCIAL—Very important to the success or failure of something.

DOMINATED—Controlled with great power.

INSPIRED—Urged or influenced someone to do something.

INVEST—Risk money hoping to make a profit.

LAWYER—A person who is an expert in the law.

LOGO—A company's official picture or symbol.

LUXURIOUS—Providing great comfort.

MOTIVATING—Inspiring someone to action.

PRECISE—Done in an exact way.

RELIC—Something that has survived from the past.

SPECTACULAR—Amazing or marvelous to see.

STANDARD—Something that is used as a guide or a goal.

TAILBONE—The bone that protects the base of the spine.

TRADITION—A belief or custom that is handed down from generation to generation.

TRIUMPHED—Won a competition.

VAPORIZE—Turn into water.

Places to Go

ON THE ROAD

DOLPHINS STADIUM
2269 Dan Marino Blvd
Miami Gardens, FL 33056
(954) 452-7000

THE PRO FOOTBALL HALL OF FAME
2121 George Halas Drive NW
Canton, Ohio 44708
(330) 456-8207

ON THE WEB

THE NATIONAL FOOTBALL LEAGUE   www.nfl.com
  • *Learn more about the National Football League*

THE MIAMI DOLPHINS   www.MiamiDolphins.com
  • *Learn more about the Miami Dolphins*

THE PRO FOOTBALL HALL OF FAME   www.profootballhof.com
  • *Learn more about football's greatest players*

ON THE BOOKSHELF

To learn more about the sport of football, look for these books at your library or bookstore:

  • Fleder, Rob–Editor. *The Football Book*. New York, NY.: Sports Illustrated Books, 2005.
  • Kennedy, Mike. *Football*. Danbury, CT.: Franklin Watts, 2003.
  • Savage, Jeff. *Play by Play Football*. Minneapolis, MN.: Lerner Sports, 2004.

Index

PAGE NUMBERS IN **BOLD** REFER TO ILLUSTRATIONS.

The Team

MARK STEWART has written more than 20 books on football, and over 100 sports books for kids. He grew up in New York City during the 1960s rooting for the Giants and Jets, and now takes his two daughters, Mariah and Rachel, to watch them play in their home state of New Jersey. Mark comes from a family of

writers. His grandfather was Sunday Editor of *The New York Times* and his mother was Articles Editor of *The Ladies Home Journal* and *McCall's*. Mark has profiled hundreds of athletes over the last 20 years. He has also written several books about New York and New Jersey. Mark is a graduate of Duke University, with a degree in history. He lives with his daughters and wife, Sarah, overlooking Sandy Hook, NJ.

JASON AIKENS is the Collections Curator at the Pro Football Hall of Fame. He is responsible for the preservation of the Pro Football Hall of Fame's collection of artifacts and memorabilia and obtaining new donations of memorabilia from current players and NFL teams. Jason has a Bachelor of Arts in History from Michigan State University and a Masters in History from Western Michigan University where he concentrated on sports history. Jason has been working for the Pro Football Hall of Fame since 1997; before that he was an intern at the College Football Hall of Fame. Jason's family has roots in California

and has been following the St. Louis Rams since their days in Los Angeles, California. He lives with his wife Cynthia and recent addition to the team Angelina in Canton, OH.